# The Kudzu Monsters

## J.R. Hardin

iUniverse, Inc.
New York Bloomington

# The Kudzu Monsters

*iUniverse books may be ordered through booksellers or by contacting:*

*iUniverse*
*1663 Liberty Drive*
*Bloomington, IN 47403*
*www.iuniverse.com*
*1-800-Authors (1-800-288-4677)*

*Because of the dynamic nature of the Internet, any Web addresses or links contained in this book may have changed since publication and may no longer be valid. The views expressed in this work are solely those of the author and do not necessarily reflect the views of the publisher, and the publisher hereby disclaims any responsibility for them.*

*ISBN: 978-1-4502-3650-8 (sc)*
*ISBN: 978-1-4502-3651-5 (ebk)*

*Printed in the United States of America*

*iUniverse rev. date: 6/16/2010*

# INTRODUCTION

My story is about a family of kudzu monsters that live in the hills of north Georgia. For those of you who aren't familiar with kudzu, let me give you a brief history. Kudzu is a bean vine that is native to China. Kudzu vines were planted in Japan several centuries ago and the Japanese introduced it to America at the 1876 Centennial Exposition in Philadelphia. Kudzu grows well in the Southeastern states. The highway department decided to plant the vine on the red clay banks along the roads. The vines quickly covered the banks and began to spread over bushes and trees. A single vine can grow twenty yards long and in the summer months can grow a foot a day. Trees that were less than fifty feet high were completely covered by the vines. The leaves died and limbs were twisted and bent down. These trees took on a spooky appearance and became known to the local inhabitants as Kudzu Monsters.

Those monsters don't move around, but in my story some of them do roam the forest. They look like kudzu covered trees. These monsters protect the forest and are friends with the small forest animals. They also help people and most people never know they were helped by kudzu monsters.

# ACKNOWLEDGMENTS

I wish to thank the Institute of Children's Literature for their help in the writing of this book.

I want to thank my sister Betty Hertenstein for her contributions and editing skills.

# Contents

Chapter One  The Bear.........................................1

Chapter Two  The Highway Bridge....................5

Chapter Three The Construction Crew ..................9

Chapter Four  The Arsonist...........................15

Chapter Five  Halloween Horror ....................21

Chapter Six  The Swamp .........................25

Chapter Seven Close Encounters.....................29

Chapter Eight The Cave ...........................33

Chapter Nine  A Dangerous Journey..................39

Chapter Ten  Slave Labor..........................43

Chapter Eleven The Escape...........................47

Chapter Twelve The Battle............................51

Chapter Thirteen The Hostages ........................55

Chapter Fourteen The Chase ...........................59

Chapter Fifteen Farewell .............................63

# CHAPTER ONE

## THE BEAR

Ten-year-old Kalvin juggled a small log flipping it from his bottom arm tentacles to the upper ones. Then spun and caught it again with his lower tentacles.

"Kalvin," said Kitty. "I want you to go look for your father. He should have returned last night from his visit with Karl and Karen. I'm afraid something bad has happened to him."

"Dad said to stay with you, Mom, until he returned."

"Well the situation has changed. I think you should go find your father."

"Okay, Mom, I'll find Dad."

His eight root-like feet raised his tree truck body above the ground. His back feet bowed up like inch worms and his front feet stretched out. They pushed and pulled him down the kudzu-covered hill. Kudzu vines and leaves covered his body. The lower ones dragged the ground behind him, making a rustling sound.

Kalvin neared a road and heard a car approaching. His arm tentacles bent down and he froze blending in with the trees around him. He waited for the sound of the car to pass before he slipped into the forest. Eventually he came to a river. *There's the Etowah River,* he thought. *I'll have to cross the river using the railroad bridge.*

Kalvin approached the bridge, his round black eyes looking for any movement in the woods or on the dark green river. He touched a railroad track with a foot tentacle. *Ah, no train vibrations.* Kalvin pulled onto the bridge. He felt a small tug as one his kudzu vines caught on the bridge and broke loose. *Oh well, a new one would grow there soon.*

He was glad he was only ten feet tall. He could still cross the bridge without hitting his head on the top steel girders. *Poor Dad, he's too tall and has to hang on the outside of the structure and pull himself across. I hope he wasn't crossing the bridge and fell in. He might be miles downstream.*

Kalvin crossed the bridge and continued along the trail, enjoying the peace of the forest, until he neared a small hill. *The squirrels in that oak tree are chattering and racing along the limbs.*

Suddenly, a bear roared! Dust and leaves swirled just over the rise of the hill. A large arm tentacle rose into the air, clutching a bush, and swung it downward. Kalvin swallowed. *That's Dad's arm and the top of his head. Dad is fighting a bear!*

The squirrels scurried along the tree limbs dropping acorns on the combatants below them. As Kalvin hurried up the hill, he could see his dad pulling up bushes and throwing them at the raging beast. Kalvin turned toward a movement on his right. Two black bear cubs ran to a sweet gum tree and started climbing.

Kalvin turned again to see his father who was pushing the mother bear away with an old tree limb. The bear clamped her teeth on the branch and bit it in half.

Looking around wildly, Kalvin grasped a sturdy log in his lower arms. He moved toward the battle as the bear swung a paw and ripped a patch of kudzu from his dad's chest. The large beast stood on its hind legs, roared and raked her claws down one of his arm tentacles.

"Oh!" His father's booming howl froze the bear for a moment. His dad quickly slammed the other twelve-foot arm into the bear's chest. Groaning, she staggered backwards and fell to the ground.

"Dad, catch this log," yelled Kalvin as he tossed the heavy piece of wood. Kleatus caught the log, but not before it struck a small tree. The tree swayed back and forth and a young squirrel fell to the ground. The frightened animal raced toward the safety of a hickory tree. Once up the tree, the squirrel chattered and flipped its bushy tail back and forth.

A hickory nut flew passed Kalvin's eyes and another bounced off his head. "Sorry, it was an accident," Kalvin yelled as he pushed away from the tree. The squirrel ignored the apology and continued to bomb him with nuts.

Husky bellowing sounds came from the bear cubs near the top of the sweet gum tree. The mother bear looked up at them, gave a final grunt at the monsters and lumbered toward her cubs.

Kalvin moved over to his dad, who was examining his arm and chest.

"Did the bear hurt you?"

"I'm fine, Son," answered Kleatus. "The bear just tore a little kudzu off, and I have a few scratches. I heard the squirrels chattering as I started up the hill, but couldn't understand what they were saying. I guess they were trying to warn me about the bear and her cubs. The mother bear probably saw me as a threat and attacked."

Kalvin saw the scratches had barely penetrated his father's thick bark-like hide. "I'm glad the bear didn't hurt you and you didn't have to hurt her."

"But why are you here? Did Kandi start walking?" asked Kleatus.

"No, she's still attached to Mom."

"Why did you leave Kitty?" scolded Kleatus. "She won't move as long as Kandi is still attached to her!"

"Mom is fine, Dad. She insisted I go find you. I think she was tired of me hanging around the hill. Why didn't you come home last night?"

"There were campers near the trail with their dogs. I had to make a new path through the forest."

Kleatus turned and started down the hill. Kalvin followed him as they pushed along the path toward the railroad bridge.

When they neared the bridge, Kalvin saw a train had stopped on the tracks. Railroad workers examined the underside of a train car. A log had slipped loose from the car, caught in the bridge structure and caused a wheel to jump off the track.

"It looks like the train won't be going anywhere for awhile," said Kleatus.

"Do you think we should just float across the river?" Kalvin asked.

"No, the river bank is too steep here. We would have to float a long way downstream before we could find a spot to climb out," answered Kleatus. "We'll have to use the highway bridge upstream to cross the river."

They followed a path upriver toward the highway bridge. The trail to the highway was narrow. Kleatus pulled up plants and tossed them into the surrounding woods. Widening the path was slow going. Kleatus had to bend back branches from half the trees they passed. The highway bridge came into view about three hours after noon.

"Maybe we should wait until dark to cross?" suggested Kalvin. "I've never been across the bridge in daylight."

"It won't be dark for four or five hours. Even then, it will be risky until late at night," answered Kleatus. "If we wait that long, Kitty will be very worried. We'll have to chance a daylight crossing."

# CHAPTER TWO

## THE HIGHWAY BRIDGE

"Have you ever crossed the bridge in daylight?" asked Kalvin. "What should we do if a car comes while we're crossing? Jump off the bridge into the river?"

"I've never crossed while it was light," answered Kleatus. "We'll fall into the river as a last resort. If anything comes, let's try leaning on the bridge railing with our faces turned toward the water. Maybe the driver will think we fell off a logging truck."

"Do you think you can pick me up above your head?" asked Kalvin. "I'll get a last look around before we start across."

"Of course, you only weigh around six or seven-hundred pounds," answered Kleatus.

Kleatus gripped Kalvin under his lower arms and lifted. *My feet must be twenty feet above the pavement*, thought Kalvin. He looked down both sides of the road and the river, as Kleatus slowly turned him.

"What do you see?" shouted Kleatus in his deep rumbling voice.

"Nothing is coming down the road, but I see a boat around the river bend. There are two men fishing. They're facing the other way and can't see us. We'd better cross while the coast is clear."

They started across, Kalvin following his father as fast as his feet tentacles could push and pull him. At least there weren't any steel girders above this bridge. Kleatus didn't have to hold onto the outside of the bridge to cross the river.

The sun had been heating the bridge pavement for hours. Kalvin's feet began to burn. The two had been on the bridge less than a minute when Kalvin heard his dad fussing about the pain in his feet.

They tried walking on the tips of their tentacles. This slowed them down and caused them to sway from side to side. The two began to groan as the pain increased.

"We have other problems besides the hot pavement," shouted Kleatus. "A truck is headed toward us. Lean on the bridge railing and remember to face the river."

Kalvin copied his father, leaning on the bridge railing with a third of his body hanging over the river. *This will make it easier to topple into the water*, thought Kalvin.

Brakes squealed and the truck stopped behind them. The driver turned off the engine. A door opened and slammed shut. Footsteps sounded on the bridge and came to a halt behind Kalvin. He felt some of his kudzu vines being lifted and then dropped.

"Call your brother at the highway department," said a man.

A minute later, a woman said she had her brother on the phone.

"Hand me the phone," said the man. "This is Fred. I'm on the six-mile bridge and there are two trees on the bridge blocking half the road."

Kalvin remained motionless and strained his ear slots for any conversation. His feet were cooling off since he stopped walking. The man said he didn't know how the trees got on the bridge.

"One of them is probably less than half a ton," said the man. "The other one must weigh a ton or more. You could try dragging them with a heavy chain, but you might do better sawing them in pieces. I've got to leave. You better get a police car out here before there's an accident."

The motor started and the truck began to drive away.

"We better hurry off the bridge," said Kalvin, "before the cutting crew arrives."

"Stay where you are," answered Kleatus. "Two more cars are headed toward us."

Kalvin heard the cars slow down, drive slowly past and continue down the road.

"Let's go!" hollered Kleatus.

Kalvin was pushing up from the bridge railing when he saw a car coming with blue flashing lights.

"A police car!" shouted Kalvin.

"The patrol car will stay until the highway department truck arrives," answered Kleatus. "Hit the water before he gets here!"

Kalvin pulled on the bridge railing until he felt himself falling into the river. He splashed into the water head first and pushed downward with his right arms until he rolled onto his back. He drifted a little way from the bridge before his father flipped into the river on his back. Water splashed onto the bridge and a large wave pushed Kalvin further away.

Kalvin was facing the bridge and saw the patrol car stop. The police officer walked to the bridge railing and watched them drift out of sight.

Kalvin turned his body around with his arm tentacles so he could see downstream. *In a few hours we'll have drifted back to the railroad bridge*, thought Kalvin. *We can't go upstream because of the policeman and the fishing boat.* Despite everything that had happened Kalvin felt restful as he drifted down the river. Several minutes later, he shouted, "I see a bank with a gentle slope!"

Using his arms like oars, he began to row toward shore. Kalvin paddled under a tree limb and wrapped his upper arms around it. He pulled until his lower arms could grab the limb. In less than a minute he was standing in the river and helping his dad up. Kleatus only had two front arms, but an arm on his back helped to push him up. When his dad was standing, Kalvin pulled on the trees to help him climb out of the river.

"The forest is dense at this spot. We'll have to pull up some bushes and bend a few trees back until we get to the trail again," said Kleatus.

"I'll go first," Kalvin replied. "I can slip through the trees easier than you and I'll look for a path."

An hour passed before Kalvin found a trail and it was near dusk when they arrived at their home. He could see his mother still standing in the same spot with her front arms folded and her back arms bowed up like wings.

"I'm so glad you're back. We have a problem!" said Kitty. "A construction crew is clearing the land below our hill."

"I guess we should leave before they start up the hill," answered Kleatus.

"I can't leave until Kandi breaks loose!" shouted Kitty. "She will tear loose prematurely if I try to walk with her attached to me. You and Kalvin will have to stop the men from coming up the hill until Kandi can walk on her own eight feet!"

# CHAPTER THREE

## THE CONSTRUCTION CREW

Kalvin and his family called a meeting on their hill with some forest animals that night.

"We have to slow the land clearing until our baby is strong enough to break free from Kitty," explained Kleatus. "I'm open to any suggestions."

"The bulldozer is doing most of the clearing and will scrape the road up our hill," answered Kalvin. "We need to destroy the bulldozer."

"I don't want major damage done to their equipment," said Kleatus. "Maybe we can do something to prevent the machine from starting."

"I could chew through some of the wiring," suggested Squiggy the squirrel.

"There's a shallow cave on this side of the hill," added a rabbit. "My friends and I can dig tunnels above it. If the bulldozer goes that way, the tunnels will collapse and the machine will be stuck in the hole. The weight of the bulldozer will cause a cave-in a few minutes later."

"I don't want any humans injured!" declared Kitty.

"We need to lure the driver toward the tunnels and then chase him away before the cave collapses," answered Kalvin.

"Kalvin and I can place boulders around the front of the hill to force the bulldozer to take a route over the tunnels," said Kleatus. "But how can we get the driver off the bulldozer before the cave-in occurs?"

Just then an owl hooted and the small animals huddled around the kudzu-monsters.

"I won't let the owl eat you," said Kleatus. "I'll chase him away."

He picked up a large stone and hurled it in the direction of the owl hoot. There was a loud crash and the owl sprang into the air and flapped away.

Kalvin went with his father to find rocks big enough to slow the clearing. He was struggling up the hill with a four-hundred-pound rock when his father passed him with a boulder twice the size of the one he carried.

A family of foxes dug shallow pits for the boulders so they wouldn't roll down the hill.

Kalvin smiled as he looked over their work. "The bulldozer won't be able to get past our rock barrier."

"We still have some work to do," answered Kleatus, as the sun began to rise.

A rabbit hopped to him and said, "We're making good progress on our tunnels. A fresh crew of rabbits will dig during the day and we'll be back tomorrow night."

Kalvin watched the construction crew begin to arrive that morning. The driver tried to start the bulldozer. When it wouldn't start, he climbed down and inspected the machine. It didn't take him long to spot the chewed wires.

Late that morning a mechanic arrived and began installing new wires. Meanwhile workmen built a small shelter that had a door and windows. Several others cut and pulled kudzu vines from the hill. They began finding some of the boulders hidden beneath the kudzu leaves.

As the workmen started home, a night watchman and a large guard dog entered the little building.

Kalvin, his family and friends held another meeting that night.

"We really slowed them down today," said Kleatus.

"Squiggy, with that dog down there it'll be too dangerous for you to go near the bulldozer again," said Kitty.

"Our tunnels will be finished tonight," reported one of the rabbits.

"We can add a few more boulders to the hill," said Kleatus. "We need to be cautious and not alert the watchman. I still don't have a plan to get the driver away from the bulldozer."

"I thought of a way to scare the driver off the dozer," answered Kalvin. "Squiggy, I need you to find Sissy and bring her to the hill before dawn."

Kalvin and Kleatus worked most of the night finishing the boulder barrier that would guide the dozer over the cave.

"The only opening through the boulders is over the tunnels and the cave," Kleatus told Kitty.

"I haven't seen Squiggy or Sissy," added Kalvin. "That could be a problem. I need Sissy to scare the driver off the bulldozer."

The next morning the crew chief examined the hill with the bulldozer operator. Kalvin watched the crew chief point out a path that would take the bulldozer away from the rocks and over the cave. Kalvin heard the driver arguing with the crew chief.

"I can continue up the hill on the original path and push those rocks to the side," said the dozer driver.

"I don't want you shoving on those boulders!" shouted the chief. "I don't want any rocks rolling down the hill and injuring my men!"

"Has anyone seen Squiggy or Sissy this morning?" Kalvin asked.

"Squiggy is asleep in a tree," said a squirrel.

"Did he find Sissy?"

A rabbit pointed to a bush with his nose and said, "She's over there with her mate, Sassy."

Kalvin called to the bush, "Sissy, Sassy, come over here and I'll tell you our plan."

"Oh dear," said Kitty, as they slid out from under the bush. "I hope they don't harm the driver and he doesn't hurt them."

"Don't worry," said Kalvin, "The driver will run away when he sees Sissy and Sassy."

Nearly an hour passed before the bulldozer scraped the road up to the tunnels. The bulldozer was right over the tunnels but nothing was happening.

"The bulldozer didn't collapse the tunnels!" said Kleatus.

A moment later they saw the front end of the bulldozer sink into the ground. It stopped sinking when the dozer blade caught on the sides of the hole. The dozer treads began to turn backwards and dirt flew into the air as the machine tried to back out of the rut.

"Sissy, Sassy," said Kalvin, "make your move and hold up your tails so the men can see you."

The two skunks emerged from under his kudzu vines and scurried toward the bulldozer. The driver spotted the skunks, cut off the engine and jumped down. He ran down the hill before the skunks started spraying his machine.

"Sissy, Sassy!" shouted Kalvin. "You've sprayed enough, come on back before the cave collapses."

The back end of the dozer had only sunk a few inches by the time the driver and the chief walked back up the hill. They stayed away from the stinky machine.

"I'm not driving that dozer until it's cleaned," said the driver.

"I'll have a man spray it with soap and hose it down," answered the chief.

Suddenly the back of the bulldozer dropped out of sight. The dozer blade jumped up a little when the back end of the machine hit the floor of the shallow cave.

"Holy cow!" shouted the crew chief. "What else is going to go wrong today?"

That afternoon a man with a container strapped to his back and wearing a gas mask sprayed the bulldozer with a cleaning solution. A truck with a water tank backed up the hill and washed the bulldozer until the hole was half full of water. Several men began digging and widening the hole around the dozer.

Late that afternoon, Kalvin watched a large vehicle with a crane back up the hill. Men climbed into the hole and slid thick iron bars beneath the bulldozer. They attached steel cables to the bars and to a large hook that the crane lowered. The crane struggled to lift the bulldozer, but the machine was too heavy. While that was going on, a large bulldozer arrived, scooped up the boulders one by one and carried them down the hill.

"We'll have to dig a trench with the other dozer," said the crew chief. "The crane should be able to pull it out."

It was night before the crane was able to pull the bulldozer up the sloping trench.

"Tomorrow's Sunday," the chief told the crew. "It's just as well. The dozer needs to dry out. I'll see you Monday morning and we'll finish clearing this hill."

That night Kandi broke free from Kitty and everyone relaxed.

"I want to thank everyone for their help in slowing the clearing," Kitty told the little animals. "Kleatus and Kalvin, I'm very proud of you."

That night Kalvin told everyone how he and his dad had attempted to cross the bridge over the river a few days ago. They laughed as Kalvin described how they tried to tip-toe on the hot pavement. He showed how they looked waving their arms for balance while hollering loudly. Kandi watched him with a big smile on her face. She didn't understand all of what he said, but she giggled when everyone laughed.

Kalvin was going to miss the hill where he was raised, but he was sure he would be happy at their new location. There was a small lake close to their future home, new territory to explore and new problems to face.

# CHAPTER FOUR

## THE ARSONIST

Kalvin watched in amazement as his little sister scooted around their new home. She reached down with one of her little arm tentacles and stroked Squiggy's back as she zoomed by him.

"Why does Kandi run all the time?" Kalvin asked.

"You did the same thing when you were little," laughed Kitty. "She has a lot of energy."

"Kalvin and I are going to check out the area," added Kleatus. "We'll be gone most of the day."

"Be careful, there are humans living nearby," warned Kitty.

"We'll keep our eyes and ear slots open," Kalvin promised. "Love you Mom, bye Kandi."

Kandi stopped petting Squiggy and waved bye.

It was still early morning as they began moving in the direction of the lake. Squiggy gnawed on a pine cone as he rode on Kalvin's shoulder. "I really love the lake," said Kalvin. "The soil around the water is rich in flavor and its fun watching the ducks swim."

"I like the early morning mist surrounding the lake," added Kleatus.

By the time they reached the lake the morning mist was already lifting and the ground felt dry on this hot June morning.

"Squiggy is a good squirrel," said Kalvin. "He seems smarter than the other squirrels."

"Yes, he's never failed to deliver a message," answered Kleatus. "I'll check the area around the lake and you scout the hills above me."

Kalvin stayed in the cover of the woods as he eased up the hill. He turned to look at his father and saw him motionless. A young girl walked on the other side of the lake. Kalvin had seen her before. She lived with her mother in a house that was hidden behind the trees on the far side of the lake.

"Maranda," a woman's voice called. "We have to leave for town, come on home."

"Coming," the young girl yelled as she disappeared up a path.

Kalvin stood at the edge of the forest on a hill that over looked a dirt road. The road ran between the hill and the lake. Kleatus roamed the woods near the lake. On the road a dust trail rose and drifted in his direction. A truck came into view. Kalvin knew his father didn't see it.

The truck slowed and stopped below Kalvin. Hidden in the shadows, Kalvin watched the man get out of the truck and walk up the hill. *He's looking around for something*, Kalvin thought. He hoped his dad saw him. A moment later, the man jogged down the hill and took a jug of liquid and a stick with a cloth attached to it from behind the truck seat. He ran down into the brush below the road and looked around again.

"Squiggy, run down to Dad and tell him about the man. I think the man is doing something bad. Stay calm and talk slowly so Dad can understand you, but run fast."

Squiggy raced down the hill as the man walked along pouring liquid from the container onto the bushes and tall grass. Tossing the empty jug into the brush, he looked around again. The man picked up the stick, lit the rag with a match, took a few steps backwards and tossed the torch into the grass. A line of fire sprang up where the liquid had been poured.

*He must be insane*, thought Kalvin. *The whole forest could burn down if the flames reach the trees behind me. Mom and Kandi could be killed!*

Kalvin moved down the hill and saw Kleatus burst from the trees and hurry toward the road. The man walked backwards toward the road, watching the fire as it spread. He turned to run toward his truck and suddenly stopped. Kleatus stood in the middle of the road towering over the truck.

The man stared at Kleatus and slowly backed up. Kleatus pushed on the truck with one tentacle and pulled on the driver's door with another. With a screech of torn metal the door hinges broke loose from the frame and the tentacle that held the door whipped around throwing it fifty feet up the hill. The tentacle wrapped around the steering column and began to pull. There was the electric pop of broken wiring and the sound of metal banging together. The steering column soared uphill, past the door.

Kalvin reached the road and pushed toward the man. The arsonist continued to stare at the huge monster trashing his truck and walked backwards into Kalvin. With one of his upper arm tentacles Kalvin slapped him to the ground. The wide-eyed man lay on his back and pushed away from the monsters. Dust rose as Kleatus shuffled down the road toward them and in the direction of the fire. A little squirrel scampered across the road and dashed up the hill toward the trees.

"We need to keep the fire from reaching the forest!" shouted Kleatus. He moved past Kalvin toward the spreading flames. Kalvin turned and headed back up the hill looking for the truck door.

Spotting the door, Kalvin hurried to it and picked it up. As he turned toward the fire, he saw his dad beating at the flames with a small tree. The fire was moving between the road and the lake blown by the wind toward the forest behind them.

Kalvin looked for a spot where the road was closest to the lake. He planned to use the door as giant shovel to scrape a dirt fire break from the road to the lake. He knew he could pull up the tall bushes with his upper arms and scraped a path with his lower tentacles. This smoke made it difficult to see, but didn't burn his eyes. Kalvin could make out his dad's shape. Kleatus was being pushed by the flames closer to his break.

Kalvin finished a narrow path to the lake and began to widen the fire break. The crackle and pop of the blaze sounded louder as the flames came closer. Kalvin saw that his dad was backed up to the fire break and strained to scrape faster but his arms were tired. *If only I could bend low like the humans. I could switch the door to my upper arms.* "Ouch!" hollered Kalvin as a shower of hot sparks landed on his chest.

The heat grew hotter every second. His dad pulled up more brush to beat at the fire. Kalvin stopped widening the path and began beating at the flames with the door. The kudzu leaves on his arms began to curl from the intense heat.

"Kalvin look behind you!" yelled Kleatus.

He turned and began beating out a small fire that had started behind the fire break.

"Behind the break!" hollered Kleatus. "We've got to stop the fire from spreading to the forest."

Kalvin and Kleatus moved further from the fire. They beat out small fires that sprang up around them.

"There are too many fires!" hollered his dad.

"Dad, I hear sirens!" Kalvin shouted back.

Fire engines from the town were speeding down the road. A large truck with a water tank pushed the arsonist's truck off the road and headed toward the fire.

"We need to disappear into the woods," said Kleatus. "The men can't see us moving through this smoke."

The two monsters glided through the smoke into the woods. Safely hidden in the forest, Kalvin examined his scorched arms. He didn't look to be in bad shape. His dad looked worse. Kleatus's arms were burned in several places and kudzu vines still smoldered on the lower front of his body.

Squiggy ran toward them chattering.

"Calm down Squiggy," said Kalvin. "We can't understand what you're saying."

"The bad man is hiding in the woods at the top of the hill," squealed Squiggy.

Kalvin and Kleatus pushed slowly uphill through the trees. Kalvin glanced back toward the fire. The flames were down, and the burned area was black and smoldering. Fire fighters walked around smothering any fires that blazed to life.

The sheriff and two of his deputies walked about the hill. The sheriff studied the dismantled truck.

"I found the steering column," shouted a deputy.

"The bad man is just ahead," reported Squiggy. "He's hiding behind a large bush."

The kudzu-monsters crept up the hill behind the man. Kleatus stretched out a tentacle and tapped the man on his shoulder.

"Ach!" shouted the man as he sprang up and ran from the forest.

The deputies quickly grabbed and handcuffed him.

"Monsters!" yelled the man. "There are monsters in the forest."

"Get him out of my sight!" roared the sheriff.

A deputy tugged the man to the police car.

"The fire is out and the bad man in handcuffs," Kleatus stated. "Let's call it a day."

"Sounds good to me," answered Kalvin. "I'm ready to go home and rest for a week or two."

When he looked back, he saw the sheriff smiling in their direction.

# CHAPTER FIVE

## HALLOWEEN HORROR

Kalvin pushed along the path that led to the human community. The tree leaves had turned yellow, orange and red. He turned around to check on the progress of his parents and his little sister. Kandi had stopped again.

"Squirrel!" exclaimed Kandi.

"No, that's a chipmunk," explained Kitty.

"Quit dragging your tentacles, Kandi," rumbled Kleatus in a low deep tone known to the kudzu monsters as "low speech." Humans couldn't understand low speech words.

*Oh well*, thought Kalvin, *we don't want to arrive there before dark.* He remembered when his dad had taken him to see the humans for the first time. He'd told him, "Kalvin, we need to stay hidden from humans. They are afraid of us and will run screaming if they see us moving."

As the sun was setting, Kalvin glimpsed the lights of the community. He didn't see anyone close and motioned the rest of the family to join him.

The others pushed up the hill overlooking the houses. Together they crept closer to the neighborhood until Kleatus saw people moving.

"A lot of humans are out walking tonight," Kleatus noted.

"Look at the children!" exclaimed Kalvin. "They've changed color and some of them have horns and wings."

"They're wearing costumes," answered Kitty. "It must be that time of the year when the children wear masks and knock on doors. The adults in the houses put candy in the bags the children carry."

They stood and watched the humans for several minutes. The excited children ran from house to house and a few adults trailed behind them.

"Kandi, the children don't normally dress this way," Kleatus explained.

He looked around. Kandi was missing.

"Kandi, where are you?" shouted Kleatus.

"Kandi, if you are hiding from us, you had better show yourself right now!" Kitty demanded in a stern voice.

Kalvin pointed, "I see her. She's headed up the road toward the human houses. I guess we didn't tell her not to play with the human children."

"Kalvin you're smaller and there's less chance the humans will spot you. Go get her before she's seen!" cried Kitty.

Kalvin pushed through the woods, keeping one eye on Kandi. *Good, she'd stopped. Its good young kudzu monsters have more leaves; it'll be hard for the humans to spot her.*

Kandi picked up a paper sack and dumped the contents onto the ground. She ran straight for a group of children, Kalvin's heart sank. He couldn't catch her in time! What would he do if the children started screaming? *If I charged out there and grabbed her, they'd scream a lot louder.* Kalvin moved through the trees tracking Kandi.

A young boy in a cowboy costume stared at Kandi as she moved toward him.

"Who are you?" asked the cowboy.

"Kandi," replied his little sister.

*Good, her high-pitched voice sounds like the human children. It's a good thing her cloak of kudzu leaves cover her feet. They'd freak out if they saw her feet tentacles.*

"What are you supposed to be," asked the cowboy, "a bush?"

"I'm a kudzu monster," answered Kandi.

More children walked up to Kandi and the cowboy. A woman walked behind them. Everyone stopped and stared at Kandi.

"Her name is Candy and she's a monster," said the little cowboy.

22

"Look at her trick-or-treat bag," said a girl in a Fantastic Four outfit. "She has a MacDonald hamburger sack."

"Yeah, but that's a wicked costume," said a small Jedi-Knight.

"Who is your mother?" asked the woman.

"Kitty," replied Kandi.

"Come on, let's go," said an older boy made up to look like a vampire.

"Wait a minute," said the woman, "Maranda is still at that last house."

*It looks like the same girl that lives near the lake,* thought Kalvin.

He watched the children run to a house and ring a bell. He moved in the shadows and tried to think of a way to lure Kandi away from them.

"Trick or treat," yelled the children. A woman opened the door and seemed delighted with all the children's costumes. Her husband stood behind her with a basket full of candy.

The woman began dropping candy into the bags and containers that the children held. Kandi held up her sack and the woman dropped in some hard candy.

*She can't eat that,* thought Kalvin. *She doesn't have teeth or a stomach and she can't absorb them through her feeder roots.*

The man and woman stared at Kandi.

"Who is this?" asked the woman in the house.

"Her name is Candy," said the other woman with the children. "I don't know where she lives and I don't know her mother."

"Where do you live?" asked the woman in the house.

Kandi pointed toward the forest.

"That's some costume," said the man. "I love those green eyes."

Kalvin looked around, desperate to focus their attention on something else and grab Kandi. He spotted a metal trash can at the side of a house. He hated to destroy people's property, but he needed a diversion. He moved from the shadow of the woods to the side of the house. His lower right arm tentacle snaked around a half-full trash can and lifted it to his upper arm. He stretched his arm tentacle behind his body and threw the trash can. It sailed over an oak tree and crashed onto the empty street.

There were screams and yells from the people and a trash can lid rolled down the street. The woman with the children shone her flashlight on the smashed can and scattered trash.

"Who the heck is responsible for that?" shouted the man in the house.

"I bet it was the Locklear twins!" yelled his wife. "Those boys are always into some kind of mischief."

"Kandi, come here to me," grumbled Kalvin in low speech. Kandi looked at him and began moving toward him. The adults continued to shout and searched the oak tree with their flashlights.

"What's making that sound?" A little boy in a bumble bee costume asked his older brother.

"I don't know," answered a pirate standing next to him. "It sounds like moaning coming from the woods."

"It's probably a zombie," said the vampire.

"What's a zombie?" asked the bumble bee.

"I'll tell you later," answered his older brother.

Kalvin snatched up Kandi and headed toward the dark forest. A German Shepherd ran to the edge of a chain link fence and began to bark. The dog's bark caused the children to jump. The vampire spilled his candy on the street and shouted that no one was to touch his candy.

*I need to get Kandi to Mom and Dad before they decide to come investigate,* Kalvin thought.

Kandi, nestled in the crook of Kalvin's arm, examined the candy in her bag. She kept the wrappers and let the candy fall to the ground. Kalvin spotted his parents hugging each other with their front arm tentacles. Kleatus was patting Kitty with his back arm and Kitty's back tentacles quivered like flapping wings.

"Mom, Dad," shouted Kalvin. "I have Kandi, she's okay."

Kitty rushed to them and pulled Kandi to her. "Thank you, Kalvin, you did a great job."

"What was that crash about?" asked Kleatus.

"I'll tell you later," answered Kalvin. "Can we go home now?"

"That sounds like a good idea to me," added Kitty.

# CHAPTER SIX

## THE SWAMP

Winter had come and gone. Kalvin felt restless as he glided about their new home with Kandi close on his feet tentacles.

"Mom, why is Kandi always following me?" Kalvin asked.

"Kandi adores you, Kalvin," answered Kitty. "She wants to be with you."

"Now that spring is here again, I want to explore the forest. But she keeps begging me to take her to spy on the young humans."

"She does seem obsessed with humans," his mother agreed. "Where do you want to explore, Kalvin?"

"I thought about going to the swamp."

"That will be a nice family outing for all of us. We'll go tomorrow."

*I'll still be stuck with Kandi,* thought Kalvin as he walked away. *Guess I'll see what's happening around here.* Kalvin pushed into the forest with Kandi and Squiggy trailing behind him.

Before long Kalvin was watching over Kandi as she hid among kudzu-covered bushes watching two boys pretend to be warriors.

*I've seen those two before,* thought Kalvin. *They're brothers named Mike and Matt. They're pretending to fight monsters with their metal pipe swords and the monsters are kudzu-covered trees and bushes. I'd better get Kandi out of here before they beat on her.*

"Squiggy, tell Kandi I said it's time to leave and be careful not to be seen."

Squiggy ran over to Kandi as Kalvin slipped closer to her. He bent down a tree limb to hide behind. Kandi's feet tentacles quietly pushed and pulled her toward Kalvin. She had just slid beside Kalvin when Matt spotted them. Yelling and waving his weapon, he charged. Matt chopped at the tree limb Kalvin held. As he struck, Kalvin released the branch. It flew up, knocking the sword out of Matt's hand.

Mike ducked as the sword sailed over his head and into the bushes.

"What are you doing?" yelled Mike. "You nearly hit me in the head with your sword."

"The tree branch knocked it out of my hand," Matt replied. "Help me find my sword."

Kalvin and Kandi inched into the forest and disappeared while the boys searched for the sword.

"Kandi, you need to be more careful," Kalvin scolded. "You're getting too close to the humans. Watch them from a safer distance."

"I'm sorry, Kalvin," Kandi replied. "I'll stay further away next time."

The next day the monster family set out for the swamp. Squiggy scampered ahead of them to talk with his fellow squirrels. They would warn Squiggy if any humans were near. They were nearly to the swamp when Squiggy reported back.

"Better change your route. A man wearing camouflage clothing is hiding near the trail. My friends say he comes every day and hides in the woods. He carries a rifle but doesn't shoot anything."

"That's strange," Kleatus responded. "Tell the other squirrels to continue watching him. Kalvin and I will check back in a few days."

After another hour of walking the monsters arrived at the swamp and settled down to enjoy watching the wildlife. A blue heron flew to the top of a maple tree. An egret with its wings folded waded through the water and searched among the cattails for frogs. Deer moved through the marshy woods and raccoons hunted for crayfish.

"I hope people don't move here and fill in the swamp," Kleatus worried aloud.

"I can't believe they would destroy such a beautiful place," answered Kitty.

"I think I'll explore some more of the swamp," said Kalvin.

"I want to go with Kalvin," Kandi pleaded.

"Is it okay if Kandi goes with you?" Kitty asked.

"I guess you can come if you don't get into trouble," said Kalvin with a sigh.

"I won't be a bit of trouble," Kandi declared.

With Kandi and Squiggy trailing behind him, Kalvin strolled deeper into the swamp, until he heard the sound of a rattlesnake shaking its tail. He turned toward the noise to see Kandi frozen motionless a few feet from a coiled timber rattler. Squiggy ran toward a large pin oak tree.

"Kandi, hold still," said Kalvin. "It strikes at movement. His poison can't harm you, but his fangs could pierce your thin bark."

He picked up the rattler with a lower tentacle. The snake struck his arm, but Kalvin's hide was too thick for its fangs to pierce. He carried the rattler into the woods and placed it on a flat rock.

Kalvin returned to the swamp, only to find Kandi gone. He looked around the scattered foliage and over the calm swamp water. He let out a little groan. "Kandi!"

He listened for a reply, but only heard frogs croaking and the splash of a turtle falling off a log into the water.

"Kalvin," Kandi's voice rang out.

Her voice came from the tall pin oak tree that Squiggy had climbed. Kandi was in the tree, her arm tentacles wrapped around a limb and hanging high above his head.

"Kandi, get down from there!" shouted Kalvin. "Kudzu monsters don't climb trees."

He pushed under Kandi and reached up with his top arms. Kandi squealed with delight and began to slide her tentacles along the limb moving away from him.

*At least she's hanging over the swamp water,* thought Kalvin. He eased into the water to follow Kandi and his feet tentacles sank several inches into the marshy soil.

*The suction of the mud is making it difficult for me to lift my feet and Kandi is inching further away.*

The limb began bending down as Kandi continued toward the end of the branch.

"Kandi stop moving!" shouted Kalvin. "The limb might break!"

The limb forked and Kandi chose the branch with the smaller thickness. It bent low enough for Kalvin to touch Kandi's feet. Suddenly, there was a loud crack and Kandi swung down in front of him. She lost her grip on the limb and fell between his upper arms. Kalvin reached out with his lower arm tentacles and caught her. Stretching as far as he could reach, Kalvin placed her on the firm ground.

"Don't go anywhere, Kandi."

He pushed and pulled through the thick mud as he slowly advanced toward the shore.

"I see you managed to get yourself stuck in the mud," hollered Kleatus.

*Oh great,* thought Kalvin, *Mom and Dad show up when I'm stuck in the mud and Kandi is standing on the ground nice and dry.*

When he pulled out of the marsh, his feet were caked in mucky gook.

"If you are through playing in the mud," said Kitty. "We should head home."

On the way home, a squirrel reported that the man was still watching the trail.

*I wonder what he's doing,* thought Kalvin. *He's wearing clothing to help him hide and he carries a rifle, but isn't hunting. If he isn't hunting, who's he hiding from?*

# CHAPTER SEVEN

## CLOSE ENCOUNTERS

"Kalvin, take me into the woods where I can watch the young humans," begged Kandi.

"I'm tired of taking you to spy on the humans," snapped Kalvin.

Kandi turned and replied, "I may just go by myself." She turned and glided away.

The next morning Kalvin spotted Kandi heading into the forest. He followed with Squiggy riding on his shoulder. Kandi found the kudzu patch where the boys liked to play. They weren't there but Kalvin saw a woman cutting kudzu vines. The woman put the cut vines into a bag and came closer to where Kandi was standing.

Kalvin had seen that woman before. She made baskets from the vines. She walked next to Kandi. He was sure Kandi's vines were too short for her to use. He hoped Kandi didn't panic.

Kandi held perfectly still with her eyes closed while the woman gazed at her vines. She examined the vines for a few seconds then walked away. When the woman walked out of sight, Kandi hurried into the forest.

"Squiggy, please come down from that hickory tree." requested Kalvin. "I have a mission for you."

Squiggy climbed down the tree and up to Kalvin's shoulder.

"Squiggy follow Kandi and keep an eye on her. Warn her if you spot any danger."

Squiggy finished munching on a piece of nut and scurried away in the direction Kandi was heading.

Kalvin followed them heading down the hill toward the lake. He knew Kandi was headed to the house where the human girl lived. She couldn't stay away from the human children, but she was growing up fast. She was over three feet tall, knew the forest and knew what to do when danger approached. Being a creature of the forest, you had to be a fast learner.

Kandi hid among some bushes and watched the girl Maranda toss pieces of wood into a stream. Squiggy foraged for food a few feet away.

Suddenly Maranda squealed. She had slipped from the bank and toppled into the water. Kandi left the cover of the forest and hurried toward the spot where Maranda had fallen.

"Kandi, stop!" shouted Kalvin. "The water isn't deep enough to drown her and the current is too weak to carry her away."

But Kandi kept up her rapid pace. Then she froze. A wet Maranda waded through the water looking for an easy path up the bank. Maranda pulled on a tree limb close to Kandi to help her climb.

Kalvin sighed with relief that she hadn't pulled on Kandi. Maranda would have pulled her off the bank.

Shivering, Maranda started toward her house. Kandi inched closer to the forest. Maranda unexpectedly stopped, turned and stared hard at Kandi. Then the sound of running feet interrupted her thoughts. Mike and Matt burst out of the woods and ran to Maranda.

"There's a rock funnel at the top of a hill that goes down about ten feet!" exclaimed Mike. "At the bottom side of the funnel is a cave opening. We went home and borrowed Dad's flashlight and explored some of the cave. It's really neat."

"It's scary too," added Matt. "What happened to you?" he asked Maranda. "Did you go swimming in your clothes?"

"No, I fell off the bank," Maranda sharply replied. "I need to change. I'm freezing to death."

"We're going back to the cave tomorrow," said Mike. "Do you want to come?"

"Sure, I'll bring an extra flashlight," answered Maranda.

"Wear old clothes," shouted Mike. "It's muddy in the cave."

The brothers walked away, Maranda ran to her house and Kandi eased into the forest.

"Kandi, why didn't you stop when I shouted?" asked Kalvin.

"I thought she might be hurt," answered Kandi.

"Maranda is bigger than you," yelled Kalvin. "She can take care of herself without your help."

"She could have hit her head on a rock," Kandi replied.

On the way home, Kandi stared at the ground and didn't say anything. Kalvin began to feel bad.

"I'm sorry I yelled," said Kalvin.

"I'm not mad at you," Kandi replied. "I've been worried I won't grow any more arms. I only have two and I want more, like everyone else."

"Your human friends only have two arms," answered Kalvin.

"I know," said Kandi, "but you and Mom have four and Dad has three."

"Don't worry about it, Kandi. I was a year old before my lower arms started to grow."

Kandi looked up at him and smiled.

"Why are you so interested in watching humans?" asked Kalvin.

"I just like watching them play," answered Kandi. "Maranda is my favorite because she's more like me."

"How is she like you?"

"We're both female and we're both brown."

"You're green," Kalvin corrected.

"I'm brown underneath my leaves," countered Kandi.

"You could pass for sisters," answered Kalvin with a smile.

"You're teasing me. I know I don't look like a human."

Kalvin hugged his sister. Kandi reached up and held on to Kalvin's lower left arm tentacle as they walked toward home. Squiggy rode on Kalvin's upper right shoulder and munched a nut.

That night Kalvin asked his parents, "Do you know of a cave on top of a hill near here?"

"I've heard of a cave on a hill," Kleatus answered. "It's too small for us to enter and the animals say it's dangerous."

"I'll ask around tomorrow," Kalvin said. "Maybe some of the forest animals know more about it."

31

# CHAPTER EIGHT

## THE CAVE

Early the next morning Kalvin, Kandi and Squiggy walked to a hill that overlooked Maranda's house. Along the way Kalvin asked the forest creatures if they knew of the cave.

Mike and Matt arrived later that morning and entered Maranda's house. While Kalvin waited for them to come out, a rabbit ran up to him.

"I talked with a gopher that knows of the cave," reported the rabbit.

"What did he say?"

"He said the cave was bad, that big rocks fall from the ceiling and there are deep pits in the ground," answered the rabbit.

"We have to stop them from going in the cave!" Kandi squealed.

"Do you know how to find the cave?" Kalvin asked the rabbit.

"The gopher said the cave is on rock hill," answered the rabbit. "But I don't know how to get there."

"I know rock hill," said Kalvin. "It's nearly a mile away using the trail and half that through the forest. We need to get there ahead of them and I'll block the cave entrance with some boulders."

"Oh look," said Kandi. "Squiggy is returning with a fox."

"Squiggy, Kandi and I are going to rock hill and seal the cave entrance," said Kalvin. "I need you to watch the house and tell me when the humans leave."

"I don't know where rock hill is located," answered Squiggy.

"I know the hill," replied the fox. "I'll find you when they leave."

Kalvin turned to Kandi. "I'll make better time if I carry you."

"I may be too heavy," replied Kandi. "I've grown a lot in the past eleven and a half months."

"Oh, I think I can manage to carry you okay." Kalvin lifted her and hurried down the hill.

Kalvin splashed through a stream and plowed through the forest undergrowth as he raced toward the hill. He spotted the fox running toward him, his bushy red and white tail held high.

"The humans are close behind me!" shouted the fox. "They're coming up the hill, now."

"I'm sorry, Kandi," said Kalvin. "I don't have enough time to plug the opening. We'll hide and hope nothing bad happens. I'll fill the opening with boulders after they leave."

Kalvin could hear them approaching. The boys talked excitedly as they hurried to the cave.

"After we crawl through the cave opening we'll be in a large cavern. At the back of the cavern is another small opening we have to crawl through," Mike explained to Maranda. "Once we crawl through that opening the cave heads downward."

"Yeah and there's a deep pit we have to cross," exclaimed Matt.

"The pit is like a split in the cave floor," Mark added.

"It sounds like you're talking about a crevice," Maranda responded.

"It's easy to cross. There are lots of rocks sticking out of the sides for climbing down and back up," replied Jeff. "We didn't go far past the crevice."

Kalvin watched the humans climb down the rocks and enter the cave.

"Squiggy, go into the cave and tell me what they are doing," asked Kandi.

"I'm not going in that cave," answered Squiggy. "I'll go find a rabbit to go in there."

"I'll go in the cave," volunteered the fox.

"Thank you, Mister Fox," shouted Kandi, as the fox crept through the opening.

Several minutes later, Kalvin felt a vibration in the ground.

"What's that?" inquired Kandi.

"I don't know," answered Kalvin. "Maybe the fox will know."

Kalvin waited for what seemed a long time before the fox came out of the cave.

"The humans crawled through an opening and a rock fell blocking the way out," reported the fox. "There is a small crack in the opening and I heard the boys arguing. They can't move the rock. They're trapped in the cave."

"What about Maranda?" Kandi cried.

"I didn't hear the girl," the fox responded.

"Oh, we've got to help them, Kalvin," Kandi pleaded

"We'll get them out, Kandi," answered Kalvin. "I'm sure Maranda is okay; don't worry about her. Does anyone know of another entrance into the cave?"

"There is a crack in the side of the hill that leads into the cave," said a gopher that had joined the group.

"Can you take us to the opening?" Kalvin requested.

They followed the gopher down the hill to a large rock with a split that opened into the cave.

"The split is too narrow for the humans to pass through," said Kalvin. "We'll have to make it wider. Mister Gopher, would you consider going into the cave to find them?"

The gopher nodded and scurried through the crack. Kalvin pulled a rock loose and began to dig around the opening.

"I'll help you," exclaimed Kandi. She pulled at a stone, but couldn't budge it.

"It would be better if you didn't work below me," said Kalvin. "A rock fragment might fall on your head."

Kalvin was pounding on the opening with a large rock when he heard the gopher squeaking for him to stop.

"I found them," the gopher told them. "One of them shined a light in my eyes and screamed. All of the humans are okay. The girl was sitting on a rock and the boys were fussing at each other. I'll go back and report if they start moving this way."

"Thank you," shouted Kandi as the gopher disappeared into the dark.

"The opening is a little wider," Kalvin said. "I'll keep chipping at the rock."

"Maranda," Kandi shouted into the cave.

Good idea thought Kalvin. They might hear her.

Kalvin chipped and Kandi yelled for what seemed a long time before the gopher returned.

"The humans are headed this way," squeaked the gopher. "I could hear Kandi's yelling and your rock banging echoing through the cave."

"We better hide in the woods," said Kalvin.

He watched as a very dirty Maranda squeezed through the opening. A few minutes later Matt wiggled out, his clothes, hands and face covered in mud.

"Look, Kandi," whispered Kalvin. "The boy is brown like you."

Kandi just looked up at her brother with narrowed eyes.

Mike had his head and one shoulder out before he stopped.

"I'm stuck," screamed Mike. "Maybe you can dig away enough dirt for me to crawl out."

"Come on Matt, let's look for something that we can use to dig," Maranda said.

They walked toward the woods. Matt said, "I thought I heard someone calling your name, Maranda."

"I did too," Maranda answered. "But I don't see anyone."

"Kandi, you better hide behind me," Kalvin whispered. "I don't want Maranda to see you."

Matt found a pointed stick and started scraping dirt from around the cave opening. Maranda had moved closer to where Kalvin and Kandi were hidden. She picked up a stick, then bent down and picked up some kudzu leaves. Kalvin noticed she was following a trail of kudzu leaves that led straight to him. He narrowed his large black eyes to make them less noticeable and watched Maranda draw closer and closer.

"Maranda, are you going to help me dig?" Matt shouted.

"I'm coming," Maranda replied. Dropping the leaves, she turned and ran toward the cave.

After much digging, Maranda and Matt pulled on Mike's arms and dragged him out of the cave.

"I wonder how far back that cave goes?" said Mike as he tried to knock some of the dirt off his clothes.

"I don't know and I don't care!" Matt shouted. "I'm never going in there again."

"Me either," added Maranda. "Look at our filthy clothes. How are we going to explain this?"

Kalvin listened to them argue as they climbed the hill and disappeared down the trail.

"Thank you, my friends, for helping us free the humans," said Kalvin.

"We were glad to help you," said the fox.

Squiggy ran toward them from out of the forest.

"My friends tell me there is a man hiding in the bushes up on the trail," reported Squiggy. "The young humans are headed away from him, but he does have a rifle with him."

"Is that the same man that was near the swamp?" asked Kalvin.

"I'm not sure," answered Squiggy.

"I'll watch him while you slip away," volunteered the fox.

"Kandi, I'll have to plug the cave entrances later," said Kalvin. "Dad and I can return tonight and pile boulders in the cave openings." As they hurried home, he wondered about the man hiding in the woods.

# CHAPTER NINE

## A DANGEROUS JOURNEY

Weeks passed and the weather got hotter.

"Kandi, you're almost a year old," said Kitty. "How would you like to go on a trip to visit our friends, Karl and Karen?"

"Will someone go with me?" asked Kandi. "I don't know the way."

Kalvin laughed. "We're all going. Mom and Dad felt you were old enough to make a long trip."

"That sounds like fun," exclaimed Kandi. "Let's go now."

"We can't go today," said Kleatus. "Kalvin and I are checking the area around our home. I had a report of a man hiding in the woods near here."

"Can I go with you?" Kandi pleaded.

"No, you stay home with your mother today," said Kleatus. "The man might be dangerous."

Kalvin and Kleatus crept close to where the man was reported to be hiding. Kalvin slowly pushed through the trees. He spotted a squirrel in a pine tree gnawing on a pine cone.

"Mister Squirrel," Kalvin whispered. "Do you see a human hiding anywhere near here?"

"Nope," he answered as he continued to chew.

"Was a man with a rifle hiding here yesterday?"

"Yep," answered the squirrel.

"What do you think he was doing here?" asked Kalvin.

"Hiding," the squirrel replied.

Kalvin returned to where Kleatus waited.

"He's gone, Dad."

"I guess we'll go visit Karl and Karen," Kleatus replied. "These sightings have me worried. I think this man or men are up to no good."

They questioned their forest friends on the way home, but no one had seen the mysterious man.

"It will take us half the day to get to Karl and Karen's," said Kleatus the next morning. "We don't need to dawdle on the way."

"Dad means you, Kandi," Kalvin chimed in.

"I'm not a slowpoke," argued Kandi.

Nobody said anything, but they all knew Kandi liked to stop and examine things.

Kandi surprised everyone by not stopping too often. Another surprise was that Squiggy wanted to go with them. Squirrels rarely ventured far from home. Kleatus led the way, with Kitty close behind. Kalvin was last, with Squiggy sitting on an upper shoulder.

They were halfway there before Kandi stopped, "Kalvin, would you look at my back?"

"Why, what's wrong?" Kalvin replied.

"Nothing," answered Kandi. "I think two more arms are sprouting on my back."

Kalvin peered at her back and saw what looked like more kudzu vines branching out.

"I see them. They could be arms. We'll know for sure in a few days." When he looked up he saw that his parents were far ahead of them.

"We need to catch up with Mom and Dad," said Kalvin.

"It's okay; they've stopped to wait for us," Kandi said as she started forward.

Kalvin looked again. His parents stood frozen on the path ahead. "Wait! They haven't just stopped," he whispered. "They're motionless. There must be danger near."

Kalvin pulled Kandi off the path and into the woods. "Be quiet, watch and listen," he cautioned her.

A man came out of the woods carrying a rifle. He talked into a device in his other hand.

"Stay here," whispered Kalvin. He slowly pushed through the forest toward his parents and the man.

The man had come up behind his parents and stood there watching them. Kalvin heard a voice coming out of the device, but he couldn't make out the words.

The man listened then said, "They aren't moving. Get here fast and bring some fire bombs."

*This is a bad man*, Kalvin said to himself. He wanted to get closer, but the forest had grown quiet. The birds had stopped chirping, the small animals weren't chattering and the wind wasn't rustling the tree leaves. He was afraid of making any noise that the man might hear.

"We're nearly there," squawked the device. "Are they still pretending to be trees?"

"Yep," mumbled the man. "They're still motionless."

The man had something in his mouth that made him slur his words and he spat brown juice on the ground several times.

*Mom and Dad are in danger*, Kalvin thought. *I need a good throwing rock.*

He reached down and picked up a baseball-sized rock. Then he heard other men talking.

Two more men stood in front of his parents and one of them held a bottle with a small burning flame. He threw the bottle at a small tree. The bottle broke and the tree burst into flames. Then the man sprayed the tree with a chemical fog and the fire died out. He walked back to the rifleman behind his parents and gave him a bottle of the flammable liquid. Now all the men carried fire bombs.

The man in front shouted, "You monsters can quit pretending to be trees and follow me. If you cause any trouble we'll burn you like that tree."

The man turned and walked up the trail. Kleatus, Kitty and the other men began to move behind him.

When they were out of sight, Kalvin crept back to Kandi. "Those men have captured Mom and Dad. Squiggy, you run ahead and tell us if any of the men turn back in our direction. Come on, Kandi, we're going after Mom and Dad."

Squiggy ran up the trail and the young monsters followed slowly behind him.

"I'm scared," whispered Kandi. "What did those men do to that tree?"

"That was fire, Kandi," answered Kalvin. "The men must know that fire can hurt us. That's why Mom and Dad went with them. Don't worry, Kandi, everything will be all right."

Kalvin wished he believed that. Too many questions ran through his head. *How did those men know about kudzu monsters? Why did they capture his parents? What were they going to do to them and how was he going to free Mom and Dad?*

The trail divided into two directions. Kalvin was trying to decide which one to take when he spotted brown juice. The man had spat on a bush on the left-hand trail. They began moving that way.

Just as he began to worry about Squiggy, he spotted the little squirrel running toward him.

"The man with the rifle is coming up the trail," squeaked Squiggy.

They had barely pulled out of sight, when they heard the man walk past them and up the trail.

"I know where the bad men have Kleatus and Kitty," said Squiggy. "They're in a stockade with the other kudzu monsters."

# CHAPTER TEN

## SLAVE LABOR

Squiggy led Kalvin to where his parents were held captive.

"Kandi, you stay hidden in the forest," Kalvin instructed her. "Squiggy, you stay with her and keep watch. I'm going to scout around and see if I can find out what's happening."

Kalvin pushed slowly through the forest until he spotted his parents standing with Karl and Karen in a pen. A rope with bells tied to it encircled the wire fence.

Walls or steel fences couldn't hold Mom and Dad, thought Kalvin, but the bells would make noise if they tried to break out.

Kalvin counted four men enter or leave by a door in the side of a hill. The door had bushes attached to it to make it look like the hill. One of the men always sat in the woods and watched the captives. The guard carried a rifle and fire bombs. The four men here plus the one on the trail made five men. Late in the day a man carrying a rifle came out the door and headed up the trail toward the sentry. Another armed man walked up a different trail. *There must be another sentry on the other trail,* thought Kalvin.

When it was very dark, Kalvin moved through the woods close to the stockade. Before he could use his low speech like he did with Kandi on Halloween, Squiggy ran up to him and sat on his shoulder.

"Kandi is in the woods behind you," said Squiggy.

"I told her to stay hidden. I wish she'd do what I said. Squiggy, go back to Kandi and tell her not to move or make a sound."

He turned his attention to his parents.

"Dad, are you and Mom okay," asked Kalvin in low speech.

The guard stood and stared at the pen.

"We're fine for the moment, but you better use Squiggy to relay messages," answered Kleatus. "The guards don't like us to use low speech."

To emphasize the point, the guard yelled, "I told you monsters not to make that moaning noise. If you don't shut up, I'm going to shoot off one of your feet."

"Squiggy, whispered Kalvin, "creep over to Dad and ask him if he knows why the men captured them."

Squiggy scurried under the fence and sat on Kleatus' shoulder. He raced back to Kalvin a few minutes later.

"Kleatus said Karl and Karen were captured this past winter when they were taking a stroll," reported Squiggy. "There weren't any squirrels to warn them, because we sleep during the winter."

"Why are they holding them here?" asked Kalvin. He noticed Kandi had crept close enough to hear their conversation.

"The men made them carry building supplies at night and clear a field to plant an illegal marijuana crop. They stood on the side trail that led to their hideout during the day," said Squiggy. "Sentries sent word if hunters or trail bikes were headed their way on the main trail. The hunters couldn't see the side trail because of Karl and Karen. The men used the supplies to build a metal building. After it was completed, Karl and Karen carried barrels of dirt from around the forest and covered the building under a mound of dirt. With bushes and small trees planted on the mound, the building looks like a little hill."

"The men are using them for slave labor," replied Kalvin. "If the building is completed why do they still need them as slaves?"

"I don't know," Squiggy answered.

Kalvin crept to where Kandi was hidden and led her further into the forest.

"Why did you follow me when I told you to stay hidden?" Kalvin said.

"I am not going to sit in the forest and wait on you to tell me what is happening," Kandi answered.

"I'm sorry I left you in the woods," said Kalvin. "I'll take you with me from now on."

"I'm sorry, too," said Kandi and she gave him a hug.

"We'll just have to watch and wait," Kalvin told her. "Maybe we'll find a way to rescue everyone."

"Karl sure is a big monster," Kandi said. "He's taller than Dad with a man standing on his head."

"Dad and Mom call him Big Karl," answered Kalvin. "He can touch the ground with three of his five arms." Then he wished he hadn't mentioned the arms to Kandi. He forgot how sensitive she was about having two.

Suddenly, there was a noise on the trail. Karl's dark shape ambled by followed by his dad. Walking behind them were two men with bombs and rifles.

"We should follow," said Kalvin.

"You go, I'd just slow you down," said Kandi. "It's okay, I'll be fine."

Kalvin followed until they passed the sentry with the rifle.

*I can't stay on the trail,* thought Kalvin. *I'll have to circle through the woods to get past him. I should have taken Squiggy to keep tabs on where they are headed.*

Kalvin hurried around the guard as fast as he could go. He used his arms to pull on trees as his feet pushed and pulled him along. By the time he returned to the trail he had lost them. He speeded up trying to catch them.

A couple of hours passed and they still weren't in sight. *What if they doubled back when he'd circled the sentry? They could be behind him. Should he keep walking or turn around and go back?* Home wasn't far. He was getting close to the lake where Maranda lived.

Suddenly, he saw Karl's shape on the dirt road near the trail. He was pulling a wagon full of steel beams and metal sheets. Kleatus was pulling a second wagon filled with bags of concrete and lumber. The men followed behind them.

"You monsters better move faster if you know what's good for you," one of them shouted.

Kalvin watched them pull off the road and onto the trail. Kalvin began retracing his steps back toward the camp. He was far enough ahead of them that they couldn't see him.

Dawn would break before he got to the hill where the sentry was hiding. He'd have to make a wider path around him. Kalvin was glad kudzu monsters could go for days without sleep. If he was human he'd be exhausted.

It was early morning by the time Kalvin bypassed the guard. He'd nearly reached the trail when he spotted Karl and his dad. Both of them were carrying steel beams. Each arm carried a beam that weighed several hundred pounds.

*I guess the wagons were too big for the trail.*

"Move those feet," shouted the man behind Kleatus and bounced a rock off his dad's back. Kleatus didn't seem to notice and continued at his same pace.

It was late morning when Kalvin returned to where Kandi was hidden. He told her what he had seen.

"I think they're building another building," Kalvin said. "That's why they haven't freed everyone."

Kalvin, Kandi and Squiggy watched the captives haul steel beams and bags of cement for several nights.

Kandi, being less than four feet tall, could creep closer to the camp than Kalvin. She listened to the men talking. Between reports from Kandi and Squiggy, Kalvin learned that the second building was a lab for making illegal drugs.

"When the building is completed and covered with dirt, they won't need Karl, Karen or our parents anymore," said Kandi. "Do you think the men will let everyone go?"

"I don't know," Kalvin frowned.

The next night it stormed and the monsters stayed in the stockade. An escape plan popped into Kalvin's head. He whispered it to Kandi and Squiggy and sent the squirrel to tell his dad. They were busting out of the stockade tonight.

# CHAPTER ELEVEN

## THE ESCAPE

Kalvin crept through the woods toward the guard. The heavy rain drowned out any sound he made. He carried a heavy stick in one tentacle and rocks in the other three. Squiggy gnawed on the bell rope that encircled the stockade while Kitty and Karen held the string of bells to keep them from falling.

Kalvin pulled closer to the guard and had slowly raised his club when a foot tentacle snapped a branch in half. Suddenly, the man rose and turned in Kalvin's direction. Kalvin threw his rocks at the guard. One bounced off his head and knocked him to the ground unconscious. Kalvin stepped out of the woods and signaled Kitty and Karen to lower the bell rope Squiggy had chewed through.

Karl and Kleatus knocked down a section of the wire fence and the monsters hurried out. Kalvin started pulling up bushes to make a trail through the woods, not wanting to use the trails where the men were hidden. The others joined him and widened the path. Karl was last since his body was the widest. Karl moved slowly as he pulled up bushes and bent back trees. A trail of kudzu leaves, broken vines and trampled bushes marked his path. Kalvin rushed toward Karl to help him.

"There's a wide stream up ahead," Kalvin informed the others. "Kandi and Squiggy are waiting there. We'll move faster traveling down the stream and won't leave a trail."

Karl began pushing through the trees at a faster pace. In his haste he plowed into a large dead pine tree and sent it crashing to the ground.

Everyone stopped and Kalvin crept to where he could see the hideout. A man stood in the doorway with a flashlight in his hand. Kalvin turned to look at the other monsters. He could barely see them as they slowly slipped deeper into the forest.

The man shone his light on the unconscious guard and shouted, "Louis is dead or unconscious and the monsters are gone!"

Two other men came out with flashlights, rifles and firebombs. The one Kalvin knew as the boss picked up his communicator.

"The monsters have escaped," he shouted into the device. "Keep your eyes open and join us in the camp."

A few minutes later lights shone down the trails as the sentries returned. The drug dealers ignored the unconscious guard lying on the wet ground and began their search. The rain was slower and sounds began to carry further.

"There's a new path over here," one of the men shouted.

The five men with flashlights, rifles and fire bombs quickly moved up the new trail.

"We can't make it to the stream before they catch us," said Karl. "Let's make a fight of it."

"No," Karen objected. "Those fire bombs could destroy the forest. Let's scatter and join up at the stream."

The monsters began pushing and pulling in separate directions. Kalvin was well hidden as he watched Karl struggle through the woods.

In a short time the men found Karl. They surrounded him and ushered him out of the forest toward the enclosure. Kalvin's parents and Karen stopped their movements.

The boss shouted into the forest, "You monsters come back here or we'll burn the big guy!"

The sentries walked up the trails shouting the same message. Karen was the first to return, followed by Kleatus and Kitty. Kalvin wasn't sure the guard had seen him, so he watched and remained hidden. The boss slapped the unconscious man across the face until he woke up.

"Louie, which monster knocked you out?" asked the boss.

48

"I don't know," answered Louie. "Something flew out of the forest and hit me on the head. We ought to burn the lot of them."

"We still need them to haul dirt and help carry the marijuana," the boss replied. "I don't know how they sawed through the bell rope, but from now on we'll have two men guarding them."

Kalvin slipped into the forest to where Kandi and Squiggy waited. "The others were recaptured, but the bad men don't know about us," Kalvin told her. "We might have to make an all-out attack on the men and take our losses. If it comes to a fight I want you to stay out of it. You're still too small to take on a grown man."

"I won't try to slug it out with any of the bad men," Kandi replied.

*I hope she means it. Mom and Dad would never forgive me if Kandi was killed or badly injured.*

"Let's continue to watch and listen," instructed Kalvin. "But don't get careless. We don't want to get captured."

A few days later, Kalvin listened to two men discussing the advantage of using kudzu monsters over mules, when he felt Squiggy climb on his shoulder.

"Kandi needs to talk to you as soon as you can slip away," Squiggy chattered in his ear slot.

When the men walked away, Kalvin crept to their meeting place. Kandi hurried to him and began talking before Kalvin could ask any questions.

"The men plan to kill everyone when the work is finished!" Kandi cried.

"Tell me what you heard," Kalvin prompted.

"The man you hit with a rock wanted to know when he could torch the monsters. The boss told him he could do it when the monsters finished pouring dirt around the lab and the marijuana was loaded on the truck. Then the monsters would be destroyed. The boss told him they would herd the monsters to the rock-covered hill. They plan to surround them and throw fire bombs at them. The boss said the fire would be contained on the rocks and their buildings would be safe. If any monster headed for the woods, they would shoot off their feet tentacles."

"Mom, Dad and the others won't try to escape to the forest if they are on fire," Kalvin said. "They will stay on the hill and throw rocks at the men until they're consumed by the flames. They won't endanger the forest. We need to act soon. The marijuana is being harvested and dirt is being dumped on the lab as we speak."

# CHAPTER TWELVE

## THE BATTLE

Kalvin watched his mother and Karen carry the marijuana crop in two large nets. They were headed up the trail followed by two guards. Kleatus and Karl were in the forest guarded by the boss and one other man.

"We need to act now," Kalvin declared to Kandi. "We'll follow Mom and Karen. We need to take out their guards and free the others."

The first man he needed to take care of was the trail sentry. Kalvin had a plan.

"The sentry is just at the top of this hill," Kalvin told Kandi and Squiggy. "Squiggy, round up some of your squirrel buddies and fake a fight in front of the guard. I'll attack him from behind. Kandi, you gather some vines to tie his feet and hands."

Kalvin noticed night was near as he crept up the hill. He gripped his club tighter when he saw the guard's back. Squiggy and two other squirrels began chattering loudly and racing around a tree. Three other squirrels joined in the fake fight. Leaves and twigs tumbled from the trees and the chatter grew louder and louder. Squiggy chased a squirrel down the tree. They flipped their tails around and jumped into the air. The sentry watched in amazement. Kalvin slid behind the man and bopped him on the head. He was still unconscious when Kandi arrived with the vines.

"Kandi, you're better at tying knots than I am," said Kalvin. "Tie his hands and feet, I'll carry him deep into the woods where he can't warn the other men. Squiggy, ask some squirrels to follow me and guard the man."

Kalvin picked up the bound man and carried him away from the trail. The man's eyes opened and he started to scream.

"Stay quiet and don't struggle," Kalvin told him, "or the squirrels will start biting you." Kalvin left him surrounded by several squirrels.

*This full moon makes it easy for me to see down the trail,* thought Kalvin as he returned to the top of the hill.

"I'm going to hide behind this tree," Kalvin told them. "Kandi, find a strong stick and hide over there on the other side of the trail. Squiggy climb up on my shoulder. I'll be able to see Mom and the others long before they get here." Thinking of his mom, Kalvin remembered that he had asked Kandi to stay out of the fight and now he was depending on her for help.

They waited most of the night before Kalvin spotted Kitty, Karen and their guards headed his way. The nets were empty and slung over their shoulders. Kalvin sent Squiggy to tell them of the impending attack.

"Kandi," Kalvin whispered. "Clobber the man closest to you and I'll get the other man."

A few minutes later, Kalvin saw Kitty glide past, followed by Karen and the guards.

A stick swung out of a bush and struck a knee cap. The man cried out in pain and hopped around holding his knee. The other man was reaching for a fire bomb when one of Karen's arms slammed him against a tree. He slid down the bark and lay unmoving on the ground. The other man stopped holding his knee and reached for a fire bomb. Kalvin moved from behind the tree throwing rocks at him. The man ducked the flying rocks and was trying to light his bomb when Kandi hit him over the head with her stick.

It didn't go exactly as Kalvin had planned, but it worked. Before long all three men were tied up and hanging from a tree in one of the nets. More squirrels had arrived to help guard the men. The squirrels screeched and bared their teeth every time one of the men moved. Kitty kept hugging Kalvin and Kandi.

"We need to hurry and free Dad and Karl before these men are missed," Kalvin told them.

"How are we going to do that?" Karen asked.

"I don't know," answered Kalvin. "Let's go back to the camp. Mom and Kandi can watch one trail. Karen and I will watch the other. We'll take care of the other sentry after freeing Dad and Karl."

They hurried back to the camp, hid and waited. The boss was the first one Kalvin saw coming down the trail. He walked past Kalvin talking into his communicator.

*He's trying to locate the other men,* Kalvin thought. A little later Karl passed with a large barrel of dirt followed by Kleatus carrying another barrel. The guard behind him carried a lit fire bomb.

*The men know something is wrong.* Kalvin could see Squiggy on Kleatus's shoulder informing him of what had happened.

All of a sudden, Karen came forward and threw a log at the guard. The man turned, saw the log and fell to the ground. The log missed him, but the bottle flew out of his hand and broke. Burning liquid ran down the path toward Kleatus. Squiggy barked a warning in Kleatus's ear slot. Kalvin saw his dad turn and toss the dirt from his barrel, smothering the approaching fire. The guard was getting to his feet. Kalvin threw a rock and stunned him. Karen grabbed his leg with an arm tentacle and lifted him into the air.

The boss lit another bomb and cocked his arm to throw it. He spun out of the way when Karl's barrel of dirt sailed toward him. The boss backed away and shouted into his communicator, "Louie we're being attacked by the monsters."

Kitty slid from the forest behind him. She struck his arm with a stick and knocked the bomb into the woods. It broke apart and burst into flames. Kitty coiled her tentacles around the boss and pinned his arms as she picked him up. Karl, Kleatus and Kalvin began beating at the fire with bushes.

"This isn't working," shouted Kleatus. "The liquid keeps reigniting the flames."

Kandi came out of the hill with a fire extinguisher. Her small arm tentacle pulled the trigger and a white fog covered the fire.

When the fire was out, Kandi said, "I found the fire extinguisher in their lab. There were lots of chemicals stored in there. I think they were already making illegal drugs."

The men were transferred to Karl. He held both of them as Kandi began tying them with the rope that held the bells.

"Kalvin and I are going up the trail to search for that last man," said Kleatus. "Kitty, you and Karen can retrieve those other three and bring them here."

Five men captured and one to go. They moved up the trail knowing the sentry didn't carry a bomb, but still had a rifle. Squirrels fanned out to search for the last man.

They were a good distance up the trail when Squiggy came running through the woods toward them.

"The bad man is past you and is hurrying through the forest toward the camp!" barked Squiggy.

"We need to return before he can free the other men," said Kleatus.

"Squiggy," urged Kalvin, "run and tell Karl the man is headed toward them."

When they were a short distance from the camp, Kandi glided up the trail toward them.

"The man didn't try to free his friends," said Kandi. "The squirrels told us that he crept past the camp through the woods and is headed toward Karen and Kitty. Karl is afraid they might be in trouble."

"Kalvin, you and Kandi stay here and guard the men," Kleatus directed. "Karl and I are going to help Kitty and Karen before that man can free the other criminals."

# CHAPTER THIRTEEN

## THE HOSTAGES

Early the next morning, Kleatus and the others arrived back at the camp with their captives.

"The last man didn't try to free his friends," Kleatus said.

"I guess he was just concerned about himself," Kalvin responded.

The five gangsters were soon hanging in the two nets that Kitty and Karen used to carry the marijuana.

"Karl, you and Karen guard the drug dealers," said Kleatus. "My family and I are going after the one that escaped. We'll think of some way to bring the sheriff here to arrest these law breakers."

"The man is probably long gone by now," answered Karl. "If we don't hear from you by tonight, we'll have to carry these men to the highway. We can't take care of them."

"Maybe he's gone, but Karen and I hid a lot of marijuana in the woods," answered Kitty. "He'll want it and it's too much for him to carry. He'll need a vehicle of some kind to haul it away. If we can get there first, we'll hide it and grab him when he comes for it."

Kalvin and his family set out toward the marijuana stash. Kalvin had Squiggy ask his friends if they had seen the bad man.

"The squirrels told me the man staggered past their tree a few hours ago," reported Squiggy.

"He must be tired, maybe he'll fall asleep and we can grab him before he wakes," said Kleatus.

Squiggy ran ahead to look for the man. Late that evening Kalvin saw Squiggy trotting toward them.

"What have you learned?" asked Kalvin.

"The bad man is in the house by the lake where Kandi's little human friend lives," Squiggy replied. "I saw the bad man hide in the woods near the house. When the woman and the girl drove up in their truck he came out with a rifle and took them into the house. My friends are watching and will send word if anything happens."

"I'm sorry, Kandi," said Kalvin. "It sounds like that fiend has taken them hostage."

"Kleatus, what should we do?" exclaimed Kitty.

"Let's not make any plans until we get to the house," responded Kleatus. "We should be there in less than an hour."

Just as they arrived at the dirt road near the lake a fox ran toward them.

"The man left the house a few minutes ago," said the fox. "He's in the woman's truck and is driving this way."

"Where're Maranda and her mother?" asked Kitty.

"Still in the house," answered the fox.

They hid in the woods as the crook drove past and up the forest road.

"He's going for the marijuana," said Kitty. "Kleatus and I will make a road block to stop the truck. Kalvin, take Kandi and go check on the girl and her mother."

Kalvin and Kandi hurried toward the house. The quickest route was down the dirt road, so they pushed and pulled as fast as they could. When they reached the house, Kalvin looked in the windows and saw Maranda and her mother tied to a stair banister. They were rocking back and forth trying to break loose.

"Kandi, do you think you can turn the door knob and open the door?" Kalvin asked.

"I think I can," Kandi replied.

Kalvin lifted her onto the porch and she twisted an arm tentacle around the door knob.

"The door must be locked," Kandi called back.

"Stay there; I'll find a stick to break a window," said Kalvin.

A few minutes later he returned with a stick and Kandi smashed the window. Maranda and her mother screamed.

"Kandi, knock out the sharp pieces of glass and I'll put Squiggy through the opening," Kalvin instructed. "Squiggy, find the girl and chew through the rope tied around her hands. Kandi, you watch from the woods and see what happens once they are free. I'm going up the road to check on Mom and Dad."

Kalvin traveled on the road until he spotted Kleatus carrying a huge boulder. A large pile of rocks was piled on the road next to a steep hill. On the other side of the road block was a field with gullies and thick shrubs. Kalvin turned and saw the woman and Maranda run out the back door. They rushed into the woods, but he didn't see Kandi or Squiggy.

Suddenly, Kalvin heard a loud noise behind him. He twisted and saw the truck turn off the road into the field. The truck bucked up and down as it plowed through the heavy brush. Kleatus and Kitty chased it. Bales of marijuana bounced off the truck bed. Then the truck took a nose dive into a hole and came to a stop. The man jumped out and ran to the road. He carried a rifle, but didn't bother to shoot at the pursuing monsters. He was running toward the house and Kalvin's hiding place.

*When he runs by me I'll nail him with a rock,* Kalvin thought. He looked in the woods but didn't see any stones. There were some good throwing rocks in the road, but he didn't want to be seen retrieving them.

Quickly he pried up a rock from the edge of the road and slid behind a tree. He heard the man's pounding feet on the dirt road and saw him streak past the tree. Kalvin cocked his arm and threw the rock. It missed his head, but struck him on the shoulder. He staggered forward, dropped the rifle, tripped and fell. Kalvin charged out of the woods. The crook looked toward his rifle, climbed to his feet and ran toward the house, leaving the rifle in the road.

Kalvin pursued him, but the man was pulling away from him. The criminal ran to the front door and unlocked it. Kalvin was still a hundred feet from the house when the drug dealer ran out the back door. He jogged toward the woods in the same direction that Maranda had gone with her mother. Kalvin noticed the man carried a steel fire poker in his hand.

# CHAPTER FOURTEEN

## THE CHASE

Kalvin twisted to pick up a stick and saw Kleatus far behind him. But as Kalvin pushed toward the woods, he lost sight of the man. He looked around for Kandi, Squiggy, Maranda and her mother. No one was in sight.

*Where are they?* Kalvin worried as he pushed into the forest.

Suddenly, off to his right he saw Maranda and her mother struggling through a kudzu field. The vines completely covered the ground, the shrubs and small trees for several acres. Kalvin watched them run and fall.

*They'll be as scared of me as they are of the man,* he thought. *I'll stay hidden in the woods and work my way toward them.*

All of a sudden, the man ran out of the forest ahead of Maranda.

Maranda and her mother turned and ran in Kalvin's direction.

Kalvin slipped through the trees until he was directly in front of them. He felt sure they would reach him before the man caught them.

Then woman tripped and fell again. Maranda pulled on her arm to help her up, but her foot was caught. The man laughed and rushed toward them. Maranda tugged at the vines until she untangled her mother's foot. Hand in hand they stumbled through the kudzu patch.

Now Kalvin could see that they'd lost too much time. The man would catch them before they reached him. Kalvin pulled up a bush and pushed into the kudzu patch.

Maranda and her mother stopped and stared. The drug dealer saw him, too. He sprinted toward Maranda and her mother, and then jumped between some bushes a few yards from Maranda. Suddenly a tentacle reached out and grabbed his foot. The man fell, twisted and tried to hit at the tentacle with the poker, but it had caught on a kudzu vine and was pulled from his hand.

It was Kandi. In all the excitement Kalvin hadn't spotted his own sister.

Kalvin trampled over kudzu vines and small bushes as he plowed through the field. The man freed his leg from Kandi's tentacle and climbed to his feet. He staggered through the kudzu vines toward the woods. Kalvin threw his bush at him. The bush hit him in the back and knocked him down. The man leapt to his feet and hobbled away.

Kalvin threw his stick and hit the man on the shoulder, but it didn't even slow him down. *He's getting away. At least Maranda and her mother are safe,* thought Kalvin, *and the drug dealer wouldn't get the marijuana.*

Just as the man ran into the woods, a small log sailed through the air and struck him across the legs. He cried out in pain and rolled on the ground. A twenty-foot kudzu monster pushed and pulled his way to him, then wrapped him securely in an arm tentacle.

*Chalk one up for Dad,* Kalvin thought. He turned and saw Kandi talking to Maranda and her mother.

Maranda seemed excited and smiled as she talked to Kandi, but her mother just stared and nodded every so often. Then the mother and daughter walked into the woods as Kandi pushed toward Kalvin.

"I think Maranda's mother is still rattled," Kandi explained. "But Maranda seems to be okay with us. I explained that our existence needs to be kept quiet. They agreed not to say anything."

"There are six drug dealers that will probably blab about us," Kalvin replied. "We'll have to move deep into the forest and hide. Where are Maranda and her mother headed and what are they going to do?"

"They saw their truck get wrecked and their phone line's been cut," answered Kandi. "They're going to a neighbor's house to call the sheriff."

"Let's look for some rope," said Kalvin. "You might have to tie the drug dealer up with kudzu vines if we don't find any."

They made their way to the house with the man held tight in Kleatus's tentacle. Kalvin found some rope and Kandi tied the criminal to a tree. Then they rejoined Kitty who was standing next to the bundles of marijuana.

"We need a plan to guide the sheriff and his men to the other men and their drug lab," said Kleatus.

"We need to stack this marijuana where they can find it," added Kitty.

"Let's leave some marijuana next to the man and make a trail with the rest of it to their hideout," Kalvin suggested.

"We need to work fast," said Kleatus, "so we can stay ahead of the sheriff and his men."

"It's getting dark," warned Kitty. "Karl and Karen will be headed up the trail with the other criminals."

Kandi borrowed a blanket from the house and they piled most of the marijuana on it. Kleatus and Kalvin carried the blanket. Kitty carried as much as her tentacles could hold. Kandi placed little piles of the illegal weed leading from the bound man to the forest trail.

"We need to hurry," shouted Kleatus. "The sheriff may be here any minute."

# CHAPTER FIFTEEN

## FAREWELL

The monster family hurried along the path, spacing the piles farther apart once they established a trail of marijuana. Squiggy was asleep on the blanket that held the marijuana. Kitty often turned to look for flashlights on the trail behind them.

It was well into the night when they met Karl and Karen on the trail. Karl had a tied up crook in each arm tentacle and Karen carried a club in each of hers.

"Let's head back to their hideout. The sheriff should be following us," said Kleatus. "We can leave the men tied up in front of their drug lab."

They placed the last of the marijuana on the trail before they reached the hideout.

"I see lights in the distance!" exclaimed Kitty.

Kleatus turned to Karl. "You and Karen take the criminals to their camp and the rest of us will place sticks on the trail pointing the way to their hideout."

Kalvin woke Squiggy who had moved from the blanket and was sleeping on his shoulder. "Squiggy, I want you to climb a tree and watch for the sheriff and his men. Tell us when they're near."

Squiggy scrambled up a tree. Kalvin made an arrow out of sticks pointing the way for the sheriff. Kleatus made an arrow further up the trail. Kandi and Kitty gathered more sticks.

"Everyone, take care not to tread on the markers," shouted Kleatus.

Squiggy ran toward them. "I see lots of lights on the other side of the hill," he squealed.

Kalvin left the last marker on the trail as lights shone down the path. All the monsters disappeared into the forest. The drug dealers were tied together in a circle on the ground.

A few minutes later the sheriff and half a dozen deputies walked into the camp.

"Well, what do we have here?" asked the sheriff. "We took one of your gang to jail. We had an outstanding arrest warrant on him."

A deputy came out of the drug lab carrying some illegal drugs. "We have enough stuff here to put you guys behind bars for years."

"I bet you're wanted for other crimes just like your friend," said the sheriff.

The deputies handcuffed the crooks and led them away. The sheriff remained behind. A few minutes later the sheriff was the only person there.

"I know you're out there," he hollered. "I want to thank you, and I'll make sure nobody believes anything those lawbreakers say about you."

When the sheriff left, Kalvin carried Squiggy to where the others were waiting.

"A lot of people know about us," said Karl. "I think we should disappear deep into the forest."

"It might be best to lie low for awhile," answered Kleatus. "Kalvin, you better take Squiggy back home. He might not remember the way back."

"I want to go with him," Kandi said. "I want to talk to Maranda again."

"You may see your friend," replied Kitty. "Having a human for a friend may benefit us."

The sun was rising as Kalvin, Kandi and Squiggy journeyed back down the trail. Squiggy was returned to his home. Kalvin and Kandi hid near Maranda's house until they saw her walk outside. Kandi glided out of the woods toward Maranda. Watching at the edge of the woods, Kalvin saw Maranda run to his sister.

"I suspected you existed," exclaimed Maranda. "You helped us out of the cave, didn't you? And you were there when I fell in the stream."

"Yes, we were there," answered Kandi. "I wanted to ask you again not to tell anyone about us. Don't even tell Mike and Matt."

"Mom and I won't tell anyone," promised Maranda. "The sheriff came by and talked to us. He said he's known about kudzu monsters for years and hasn't told anybody."

"We're going to disappear into the forest for awhile," Kandi told her. "We might be back this summer."

"Please come visit me again, Kandi," pleaded Maranda.

Kalvin and Kandi waved goodbye as they melted into the forest. They rested awhile and headed back to their parents that night.

It was mid-summer before Kalvin and Kandi were given permission to visit Maranda. They returned to the lake and waited in the woods near Maranda's house. A few hours later Maranda came out and walked toward the stream. Kalvin watched as Kandi left the forest and pushed toward the girl.

*Kandi is over four feet tall,* Kalvin thought. *She looks more like Mom with those purple and blue flowers sprouting from her head.*

Kandi was so disappointed when the growths on her back turned into more vines. He watched Maranda squeeze Kandi's arm tentacle like she was holding her hand as they talked. Her mother came out, sat on the porch and watched them.

*Mom seems okay with Kandi having a human friend,* thought Kalvin. *I wonder how Maranda's mother feels about her daughter having a kudzu monster for a friend.*

Kalvin scanned the area for other humans. He didn't see any people, but he spotted Squiggy in a tree. Then he saw Kleatus creeping through the woods. Kalvin smiled to himself. He glimpsed his mother gliding behind his father. The woman went back into the house, but Maranda stayed and talked for a long time.

"Maranda's mother has put their house up for sale or rent," Kandi told Kalvin when she returned. "She felt it would be safer living in town."

"I know you'll miss her," said Kalvin. "But I think her mother is doing the smart thing."

Kandi continued to visit Maranda during the summer when Mike and Matt weren't around. Kandi told her about kudzu monsters and Maranda told Kandi a lot of stuff about humans that the monster family didn't know. Kitty thought it was a good learning experience for all of them.

Near the end of summer Maranda came out to meet Kalvin and Kandi.

"Mom's rented our house to a man. Saturday Mom and I are moving to an apartment in town."

Tears ran down Maranda's cheeks.

"I'm going to miss you," said Kandi. "I wish I could cry with you, but kudzu monsters can't cry."

"I can't stay and talk," sobbed Maranda. "I have to go back inside and help Mom pack our things."

Maranda hugged Kandi and ran back to the house.

Saturday morning Kalvin and Kandi sat on a hill and watched men load furniture into a large truck. When everything was loaded the men drove away.

"Let's go to the top of that grassy hill," said Kandi. "We'll be able to see Maranda when she leaves."

"You go on," Kalvin replied. "I'll stay in the woods. I'm taller and can see Maranda's house from here."

Kandi moved to the top of a hill. Maranda and her mother came out of the house and climbed into their truck. Kandi waved as the truck drove away and Maranda and her mother waved back. Kalvin watched his sister wave until all that could be seen of the truck was a dust cloud on the road.

Kalvin pushed next to his sister and wrapped an arm tentacle around her. She hugged him back as Squiggy climbed down from a tree and raced around them chattering. Kalvin felt something on her back.

He smiled and said, "I'm sorry your friend left but I bet you'll see her again someday. I have some news that will make you feel better."

"What news is that?" asked Kandi.

"Those new knots pushing out on your back are turning into arms."

# THE END